AF448339

# CONDITIONS APPLY

Novella by Jasvinder Sharma

Right from my childhood I had seen my Mom struggling to keep her family intact.

Dad had no sympathy or love for her. He tried twice to  bring his mistress permanently to our home. His mistress was pitched against us and that brought havoc to the peace and tranquility of our house.

Mom pardoned Dad but after a very long time. It lost it's relevance then.

You can't grant pardon in love and no one can pardon a cheat in love. Love is either there or not there. There is no midway. There is no such state where love can be a seasonal or occasional affair. If love becomes a compromise then it is not love, it is lust in its place that prolongs a relationship.

In my parents' case, it was neither love nor lust.

Mom never called Dad's Mistress her by her real name.

She called her *she*.

Her name was Deepika. She worked in Dad's office. Dad had other charming women there to date. Deepika came and stayed very long in his romantic adventures.

Dad usually took me to his office when I was about six years old.

I remember him introducing me to his office female friends too cordially. They would welcome me with warm heart and played joyfully with me. They kissed me and gave me chocolates.

Deepika was different from all those ladies.

She would lift me, she would hug me closely and she would kiss me passionately. She was my favorite in the whole office. She would offer me coke and potato chips. I felt happy playing with her.

One day I was in Dad's office.

I was sitting happily on Deepika's lap. She was wearing a tight beautiful dress. She had big eyes and long hair. She was sitting in Dad's cabin. Dad was standing in a good mood near her.

Deepika asked me in a sweet affectionate voice, 'Kiran dear, who is your favourite person in the house.'

I readily replied, ' Dad.'

'And who else?'

'My Mom.'

She embraced me tightly and implored, 'any other person, other than Mom and Dad?'

She wanted me to tell her name. But she was not my family member.

I thought for a while and said, 'My sister.'

' Don't you like me?'

'Yes I do.'

She blushed and kissed me and asked me in a soft tone, 'Suppose your Dad come to my house and live with me, would you live with us too.'

It was quite an indecent and unfair proposal. I felt bad. Bad for my mom. How could Dad live with a lady from his office. Surely it was a bad joke.

I jumped down from her lap in panic. I could not understand what she meant.

As I grew I found Mom discussed openly about Deepika with my elder sister.

I wouldn't understand at that time why Mom disliked and rebuked Deepika. I could only guess Mom was jealous of her. Deepika was blonde, dressed fashionably, displayed jewels and loved me. I thought it was because she loved me so much and that's why Mom was worried lest Deepika may snatch me from her.

I came to know the whole matter going around Dad and Deepika when I grew up.

Quarrels of Mom and Dad became fiercer and more violent. Deepika was the center of their quarrel and discord.

Mom abused Dad alleging his wanton affairs with many ladies predominantly Deepika. Dad would swear placing hands on me and my sister. Mom didn't believe him. They would argue more and threat each other.

For days together Mom and Dad were not on speaking terms with each other. This affected me and my sister badly.

Dad's mistress had brought havoc in the house. Dad always denied having any relations with her.

Mom would spy secretly on Dad. When we went to school Mom would hire a taxi and go here and there searching his unfaithful husband.

She would catch him sometimes.

Dad was found sitting with one of her lady from office in some cafe or at the market place. Mom would create a scene there and every person in his office came to know about Dad's filthy affairs. Dad never corrected his ways. He remained a rebel and a cheat.

Back home Dad would swear again and again and for a few days he would remain sincere to Mom but again he would repeat the same story.

Then Dad made a big blunder. His casual affairs were quite harmless. Our house was intact. He got emotionally involved with Deepika a fair and smart young lady.

For Dad Deepika was a great catch but he could not swallow that catch. Deepika was tactful enough to have designs of marrying Dad. When she captivated full attention of Dad, Dad stopped being our family member.

Dad was blindly in love with that young lady. He started staying out on the pretext of tours to other cities. He would take Deepika along with him and stay in hotel there.

Dad and Deepika became the talk of the town.

One day I spotted Deepika at our door.

That was the height of her guts. She appeared at our house one afternoon, asking for my father.

I came out and greeted her smilingly. It was only I who had no ill-will or resentment in my heart against her.

I was fascinated by the slight bulge beneath her breasts.

I was aware baby grows in woman's stomach, because my mother had recently given birth to my baby brother. I was sure that Dad's friend would also give birth to a baby. I was attracted towards her.

Till now I thought her to be a close friend of Dad at his workplace in the same way we children had boys and girls as class mates.

It was quite later that I came to know that Dad made Deepika pregnant and it was a crime for a married man to do such thing. And from then onwards I started hating her because she had snatched my Dad from us.

Deepika was firm in her resolve that day. She stood at the door silently looking down. She was in her best outfit.

She asked me politely, ' Kiran, Is your Dad inside the house. Please tell him about me.'

Mom had issued strict orders to us not to tell anything about Dad to anyone from office. I was in a fix whether to tell Deepika about dad or not. I wondered why she had come to our house when Mom doesn't like and tolerate her.

I went inside and called Mom quickly.

My mother was very angry seeing Deepika at the gate. She was horrified to see her courage. Does she not know he is a married person with three children.

Mom screamed loudly at her at her highest pitch. For a while Deepika was horror-struck and trembled. She tried to say something fumbling for words but she could not say anything. She was guilty and defendant.

Deepika digested the whole insult without rising any word and she lowered her eyes, stood there gloomy for some moments and then without uttering a single word, she went away. Mom had disconnected our landline phone so she came to enquire about Dad.

That is how I remembered Deepika in my childhood. It was her beginning to ride forcibly into our house.

She had planned to take away Dad one way or the other to her home but Dad was still under the control of Mom.

Mom should not have kept Dad like this. You can't allow your husband to play double game with you. Strict action and scolding could have deferred Dad's disobedient and rebelling activities of following his fanciful misadventures.

At that tender age, I was not aware of the games and tricks the elders in my house played on each other. That was a totally different set of behavior for me to apprehend. Dad cheated and then swore he did nothing.

Mom stopped taking Dad for outdoor activities to arouse his love and passion for her. She always remained busy tending household activities and getting us prepared for examinations. They had no romantic life. Dad was energetic.

Dad needed some young doll to play around. The ladies from his office were his sweethearts and he poured all his love on them. He won't pay attention to us.

With these married women of his office Dad's family life was safe. These women just needed Dad's attention. They took lunch with him at good restaurants and got costly gifts in exchange for kisses or hugs.

But When Deepika came in Dad's life, everything was at stake. Dad was overjoyed thinking a young and beautiful lady took so much interest in him.

Dad made her the queen of his kingdom. The whole office recognized Deepika as the official wife of Dad. She commanded more respect that the Boss himself.

Dad paid all his attention to Deepika. She would sit in Dad's cabin all day. She took her tea and lunch there. On holidays, Dad would open his office because of her and both of them came so close that she offered everything to Dad.

Dad became mad finding such a passionate woman. She would sit in his lap, she would kiss him deeply and they they started having a rocking sex. Mom had no time to cajole and coax her husband. Her sex with Dad was tasteless and customary. Deepika was quite a frank girl.

Deepika was from a small town and her parents wanted to get her married to a respectable boy. They sent many prospective boys and tried their best to see her married soon.

When Deepika met my Dad, she thought of a brief flirting with him but Dad poured himself completely into her showing complete submission and after that she fell in love with him. Deepika liked mature, wealthy and influential person like my Dad.

Dad was a true bohemian and a fashionably romantic officer. He dressed like a hero.

He was romantic and crazy since his childhood. Before his marriage with Mom, he was seriously involved with his college class mate. Mom told us on one occasion. He was so mad after her that he didn't stop going to her town. She too was married but that was no hindrance for them. They managed to meet in coffee houses and cinema halls.

That was not my father's first foray of infidelity against my mother. I remember many other incidents when mother took Dad to task for his romantic involvements at his office and even with Mom's friends.

Dad would find Mom's friend an easy target to lure because these women needed Dad's help in getting some government work done easily through Dad. Dad would take them on long rides.

Mom always suspected Dad had intimate relations with other women other than his office too.

Dad was too complex a person. He got bored from one woman in one week only.

I read his diary secretly. He wrote in it sometimes. He claimed he remained with a new woman every month.

He kept a proper count of women he met. He didn't mention he had sex with all of them but it was his vanity and fancy to touch and feel and be with a new woman every now and then. It showed his perversion too.

I fail to understand how Dad got time for all these ventures. He was a responsible officer of a large office.

I think now why Dad hankered after so many women. Was there no woman who could hold his attention for long. Mom couldn't satisfy his lust. But he was deprived of love too.

Dad loved no woman seriously. Woman came and faded out of his life slowly but he kept searching a true soulmate till Deepika involved him with her.

After Deepika, Dad wrote nothing in his diary. He tore it one day. Even in Deepika too he didn't find true love. After his divorce from mom, he married Deepika unwillingly and after barely a year they started fight as Dad fought with Mom.

But this woman Deepika from his office was Dad's special girl. For her, Dad was damn crazy and later on when Mom was so much harsh against her, Dad was ready even to desert us.

Dad created such an atmosphere in the house we dreaded fight between Mom and Dad every day.

Initially they fought for hours in their bed room, then had violent sex and then they would sleep calmly. Dad was a great manipulator. He would promise a good behavior in future and took Mom to market for shopping and a fortnight passed easily.

But the frequency of their discord was increasing sometime twice a week. Mom kept abusing him and Dad threatened Mom to leave the house.

Many times Mom told me that she was leaving Dad for good but in those days of late nineties, it was not easy for a middle class woman like our Mom to walk out of a corrupt and loveless marriage especially when she happens to have three grown-up children and no income of her own. Mom's Parents too didn't back her.

Dad was a real devil. He had managed to impregnate the two women in his life within six months of each other. With Mom it was right as she was his lawful wife but where his mistress should go with a bulging belly.

Deepika was quite a daring girl to have decided that she won't abort the illegitimate baby of my Dad growing in her belly. Dad coaxed her much to get rid of the baby but she was not ready to leave Dad. Poor girl, she did not know that she was heading towards a more troubled and stormy life ahead.

Deepika was impudent and bold. Dad was in her complete grip. She wasn't about to fade into darkness or oblivion. She was 25, old enough to have known better perhaps.

So was he, my dear Dad, a married man of 40 with an uncompromising and nagging wife and three children and another from his illegal wife on the way. All this requires nerves of steel and solid guts.

Dad's young paramour was a force to reckon with. I admire Deepika's obstinacy or was it her resolve? Her mother was going to throw her out, owing to the shame and blames from the society. And my Dad was not about to abandon his wife and children.

At that period of history the term single parent was many years away. Dad and his young beloved were pioneers in that field.

Soon Dad turned indifferent. He started showing apathy to Mom and us. He was paying more attention to his beloved mistress. Dad was away from home a lot during the later stages of Mom's pregnancy. I later realized that he was with Deepika. Dad was away when Mom gave birth to my younger brother.

It was my elder sister and our neighbors who accompanied Mom to the hospital when Mom was in labour pains. Mom knew who Dad was with if not where he was: she was sure that Dad was with Deepika and her pregnant belly.

Dad turned up at home a couple of weeks after Mom gave birth to the baby boy. There was hardly any conversation between Mom and Dad. He now seemed to be from some another place. He ignored us too.

From then on Dad divided his time between the two households. If he stayed with us too long then his worried mistress would come to our house, searching and calling Dad.

And on the contrary if Dad stayed too long with his mistress, my mother didn't care much. Mom left my Dad alone because the house was so peaceful when he was not there. Mom was busier with the baby and household chores and educating and sending us to school.

Dad would come, hand over the whole pay packet to Mom and leave without any utterance or words of care or affection. For him, life was a merry go round. His mistress was earning and spending for him. It was Mom's fault to accept Dad's wayward behaviour. But what could she do?

Mom never had a fight on economic front. It was the love between them that was eroding and waning. With her own children on her side and a securely home and a handsome salary every month from Dad, Mom had given a long rope to Dad to meander here and there. And that made the matter from bad to worse.

May be in her heart, Mom was confident that Dad would mend his ways sooner or later. Had she adopted a stern attitude towards him right from the beginning, she might not have lost Dad that way. When she let him have his own way, Dad was unstoppable.

And then she lost her cool.

Dad and Mom fought physically one day. But this was not how Mom wanted it. She told many times to me and my sister that Dad wanted to hug or kiss her forcibly.

Mom was not ready to allow a person like him to embrace her. She refused and Dad held her hand with force and she struggled to get herself free and abused him loudly. Dad wanted to gain access to his lawful wife still now as much as his mistress little knowing that in love you can't woo both your wife and an outside woman equally. One has to be left out.

And she was Mom. How could she accept her husband fostering a son born by him to a woman in office. Simply impossible. How could Dad be such a fool.

And the inevitable happened.

I came home from school one day to find my mother gone and my father kneeling on the shabby rug struggling with my baby brother's nappy. He was in a very deplorable and pitiable condition.

'Where is the Mom?' I asked frightfully.

' She is Gone', he replied in a cold and dry voice.

'Gone, but where?' I demanded rightfully but in subdued tone.

'Just gone, don't know. Just go inside and change your school uniform', was his stern and angry answer.

Dad commanded the highest position in the house. A man is head of the family. His wish reigns supreme. With his income, he strengthens his position and before his growing power there lies his poor wife – his lifetime hostage and mortgaged to him by statute and tied to his house due to her love for her children.

Dad didn't tell us where Mom was.

He was in a bad mood, angry and exhausted.

My elder sister came from her school and she was horrified as me. Dad prepared food for both of us which we didn't like at all. But how could we make Dad more angry and more wretched and more miserable. We finished our homework and went out to play in the neighborhood.

The next morning too, my mother had not returned. Dad went to office taking my baby brother with him. Perhaps his mistress tended him there. Our aunt in neighborhood looked after us that night. We were worried where was Mom and whether she was alive or not? When will she come back? What will be our future now.

Next day, when I was back from the school, Dad's mistress arrived in the house along with my baby brother and her baby girl.

Deepika took the charge of our house now.

She cooked food for us and washed our clothes. She and Dad slept in the bedroom where Mom used to sleep.

Mom and Dad would sleep there without a single stroke of noise.

Now Dad and his mistress rocked the bed room. Love is not the greatest glue between two people, sex is. Dad and his mistress had both. Only my Mom was uprooted from the house.

Dad was in a high air. I and my sister were frightened at this obnoxious development in the house. We were missing Mom too much. We expected her any moment. We had no clue where she had gone. Perhaps she had run away to maternal uncle's house or Mom's sister's place.

Was she alive, we feared? From whom could we enquire? Neighbors had their own questions. Who is this woman with a baby in our house? Dad lied to one of neighbors saying she was his close relative whose husband had deserted her. We were lip tied.

My mother returned three days later.

Life returned to normal for us.

But for the elders in the house it was a period of immense turmoil and tension. We children were back to our routine – going to school, doing homework and playing in the evening. How could we interfere in the mess created by Dad?

So there we were all – one husband who was our father, two mothers and four children in one house. Anarchy reigned here 24 hours.

When Mom came back, the status of Dad's mistress diminished. Deepika would remain calm and restricted, sitting all day in the corner front room near main gate. She had absolutely no say in any matter of the house whatsoever.

Mom controlled the house from the large bedroom. Dad too was subdued. On every alternate day, the elders created raucous scenes. They abused and blamed each other and we children were getting used to such noisy brawls and scuffles.

Dad promised that he would soon pack up his beloved and the illegitimate baby. My father and Deepika didn't sleep together in our house. She and her baby slept in the front room. My father slept in the drawing room on sofa. Mom and Dad rarely spoke with each other and they occasionally communicated through us innocent children.

So there he was, with two women to attend to his needs.

The atmosphere was very uneasy and tense. Mom shunned him or I would like to think she did it to offend him more and more. But Dad couldn't get her message. She was invoking her love in his heart but Dad had become dumb and deaf for her. He was madly in love with his mistress.

Dad was adamant and unbending.

He was bent upon keeping his mistress and my Mom under one roof. It was like sailing in two boats at one point of time. Dad was torn between the two women. With Mom he had neither love nor desire for sex. He had little time for us too. We too drifted away from him.

Our sympathies were with Mom.

If Mom wept, all of us were on her side, wiping her tears and consoling and comforting her. And that made Dad more hostile towards us. He loved us but he loved his mistress more than us. Deepika was young and sexy. She was Dad's weakness. Mom didn't allow her stay in the house and Dad wanted her to stay with him at any cost.

Every night we all sat around the table to eat. There was terrible silence all around and we behaved as if we were aliens.

Every morning we snatched our bowls of breakfast cereals after taking our turn in the bathroom. Mom attended us first and when we left for school, Dad and his mistress would go to the kitchen to prepare food for themselves.

Dad had pitched Deepika and her girl here on us forcibly. The courage of Dad and his mistress was appreciable. They were living under fierce volleys of Mom's abuses and scolding.

Dad's mistress would keep sitting in her room attending to her baby girl. She was on long leave from the office. Dad was in charge there and she had no problems. We didn't play with Deepika's girl. It was forbidden for us to talk to her or to her baby. We stopped talking to Dad too. We were all one in the tirade of Mom against Dad.

In order to get majority votes in the house, Deepika tried many times to bring me to her side. She brought me a book titled *The Little Prince* on my 12th birthday.

I loved that book. I liked her gestures.

She wanted to be kind to me, I knew but I had to be loyal to my mother at the same time.

But a part of me liked Deepika when I was a kid. Later on I became more hostile to her when the condition of Mom worsened.

But I felt sympathetic for her sometimes. Why did she choose to love and marry an already married person with children. She was very attractive and smart. She could easily find a young suitor. Anyway I didn't understand the enormity of sin of what Deepika had done. She was affectionate, beautiful and loving.

Soon the break up between Mom and Dad set in. Deepika started coaxing Dad to move out of our house since Mom was becoming more violent and abusive.

One of them had to go.

Mom was not ready to surrender. It didn't become the permanent arrangement. My father wouldn't have minded but Mom was full of shame every time she wheeled her baby boy down the front path of our house.

Everyone's queries in the neighborhood made Mom feel small and insulted.

Mom tried to cover up Deepika. But she was sure that people knew the truth. We were all told to say to the people around that Dad's mistress was just a tenant.

And who cared what Deepika was. People don't care much what is going on in another house. Only Mom had to bear Deepika, share her and tolerate her in her very own house.

Mom tried all lucky charms, trinkets and every talisman. She consulted many lawyers and all renowned astrologers. She talked her heart out to her brother and sister but no way could be found to oust Dad's mistress from the house.

The only reasons why Deepika didn't move out of Mom's house might be she loved my Dad passionately. For that she remained dead silent and tolerated all ill-treatment, abuses and violence.

Months later, when my mother couldn't bear it any longer, she went to the cruelty to children organization and the Women Police cell. She reported the matter to Dad's head office too.

The Police officer came threatening. Deepika surrendered easily before them. Dad too decided not to face courts and indifferent neighbors.

Police persuaded Deepika to leave.

Deepika left our house one night. A large part of Dad also left with her.

Expenses on our studies were increasing and tension between Mom and Dad was mounting. Mom remained mum and depressed all the time. She stopped caring for herself. She never wore good clothes. She stopped doing makeup. She avoided wearing jewelry. She stopped going anywhere for fear people would ask awkward questions.

Dad was taking care of our household expenses but Mom would unleash all her anger and bitterness against Dad on us.

It was her misplaced anger. She scolded us most of the time. She blamed her pitiable state was because of us. She cried wildly and abused us saying if we were not there, she would have divorced Dad and married again or she would have gone back to her parents' home.

We were unconvinced though we felt guilty. We tried various ways to please her. Her tough attitude towards us filled us with remorse and we didn't feel obliged to her. We became confused and we started hating her.

It was killing time for Mom.

Mom was bold and she digested all the venom and bitterness that Dad showered on her. She was right and justified to some extent.

If Mom had not withstood all that turmoil and uproar in her life, we children would have suffered most. We would never have been able to get quality education from premier institutes. What my Dad did was not a rational behavior from any angle.

Keeping a mistress and that too keeping her at own home, Dad pitched an unending battle against a lawful wife and children and it was something intolerable in any society - tribal or post-modern.

Dad made four of us – Mom, we two sisters and my younger brother suffer so badly and for so long. We remained emotionally unstable and self-doubting all our life.

Many men run extramarital relations but they are clever to keep secrets. They live double lives. They keep such humbug out of their legitimate household. They don't insist their illegitimate partner would stay at their own home along with the legally wedded wife and her legitimate children.

After Dad's mistress left our home and Dad went to live with her even though for few days in a week, he became an unfamiliar strange person for us.

From then on my father was the head of two families. He stayed with us for four days and visited his mistress for three days. But now he became more cold and quite stranger for us.

I graduated from Prince College. I was looking for a job. My elder sister was a teacher in a good school. She was getting a good salary.

Dad was now completely with his mistress.

He visited us in the first week and stayed here for a few minutes. Handing over money to Mom, he would leave without asking any good or bad thing. That meant a dead end had arrived in the relationship of Mom and Dad.

And finally Mom decided for herself.

Mom had become sick of seeing a rogue coming in and going out of her house.

She was more disturbed when Dad was around. She wanted to come out of this meaningless and torturing triangle. She was tired of keeping formal relations with a person who was enjoying his life with a woman half his age but keeping his wedded wife in the storm of fire.

Mom thought - there is no chance of bringing him back. Dad had no remorse or regret. He had no affection or worry for the gloomy future of his two legitimate grown up daughters.

Mom consulted lawyers about the benefits of seeking a divorce and she was told it would give her a peace of mind and a permanent security. Now she wanted both for her at this age.

Mom filed papers for divorce in the court.

She had a slight apprehension and a faint hope that her husband who fathered three children from her, would reconcile with her.

She has a hope Dad would come forward with a proposal as not to end the relationship. But Dad was in some other world. He wanted Deepika to stay here and for that Mom was not ready.

Dad decided to live with his mistress.

After a year Mom finally divorced Dad.

The settlement was done outside the court through a common relative whom Dad had approached.

Dad paid a large sum to Mom. He agreed to pay her a sufficient monthly amount to take care of the house and children.

Mom readily signed the papers. She freed him and she was also liberated and enlightened.

My sister was in the marriageable age. Dad went to live with his mistress.

After a month, I came to know that Dad married his mistress. He was so thrilled that we were told Dad went to Europe for Honeymoon.

Having been through one failed love myself, I understand my Dad better now. I no longer blame his mistress. She was charmed by him. She loved him till the day he died. But my mother would never forgive her; nor till the day did she die.

I could not decide who was wrong. Was mom not responsible for having allowed Dad's mistress to stay at her home for nearly a year. She should have taken a strong step at the very first instance - the first day. Dad became devilish day by day when Mom became silent.

Mom was saturated. She changed her course of life. She became another woman. Dad was unfortunate. He lost the two worlds.

After his marriage with his mistress, Dad lost all the fascination and charm for her. Till now Deepika had no power and authority over him. They were just lovers living in a false romantic world.

After marriage with Dad Deepika became his wife and she started checking him and scolding him all the more. Dad was a rebel by nature. He was not a one-woman man. Deepika too failed to tame him.

Like a letter posted without postage stamp, Dad was shunted from Deepika to us. He was tossed like a tennis ball - from here to there. Now he tried to regain his lost paradise but time had changed now. Damage was already done.

Dad was a changed man now. We had a great hatred for him in our hearts.

Dad would now bring costly and gracious gifts for us on our birthdays. He would bring us gorgeous clothes and he would now enquire about our studies and careers. On the pretext of seeing us, he would frequently come to our house like an unwelcome guest.

Mom's mental position was constant but unsure.

She never spoke what she thought of Dad's changed ways. She had closed his chapter. Her hopes were shattered.

Mom lost her faith in us too.

She became indifferent.

We no longer consoled with her since we were busy shaping our own careers. When Dad had married his mistress, count down had begun on the same day for the end of relationship between Mom and Dad.

Maybe when Dad signed divorce papers everything was finished. What remains after the dissolution of a 22 years long marriage?

The answer is simple.

But Dad was so childish. When his mistress rebuked and scolded him, he turned to us to recoup what he ignored and lost but regaining lost love from children is not possible.

Mom remained firm to her resolve not to face Dad till her death.

She never uttered her husband's name after their painful divorce. She had a hope that because of her, her beautiful house and sweet and promising children, her husband would never divorce her.

Dad proved her wrong and that was all for that sexy mistress of him that he pushed Mom to this end and she never forgave him.

There was no spark of humanity or any other feeling between Mom and Dad now. They were dead for each other.

Like a pendulum Dad kept tossing from his mistress to our place now. He came to his own house now like an unwanted guest. No one liked him now.

Mom had become a rigid religious person now.

When my brother cleared his Engineering Examination, Mom became a totally devoted person.

We sisters got good jobs. My brother got scholarship from an American university for doing MBA.

Mom stopped taking interest in us. She would get her compensation amount – a large sum on 1ˢᵗ of every month. She had a house which Dad could not dare to vacate from her because we still lived in it.

Dad was becoming more and more affectionate with us. Till now he had ignored us. It seemed he was compensating us for the neglect he made in our childhood days. But now that touch was missing on our part. We never reciprocated him in that spirit and that made him try more hard to win our hearts.

Mom was becoming indifferent. She never worried we sisters were crossing marriageable age. Moreover Dad was more affectionate with us but he too never bothered to find a suitable match for us. Mom and Dad both left us on our own. We were in our early thirties.

Dad had become alcoholic now. He drank right from morning. He would come like an friendless guest. He would take lunch or dinner; he would make formal inquiries from us and leave this place without a emotion in his car.

Dad would visit us mostly on Sunday morning when either I or my sister was at home. Dad never came when Mom was alone in the house. They had become complete alien to each other. That was a height of hate and unconcern between them.

When my sister took the decision to live with her man, she entrusted me with the responsibility of briefing Mom with the entire affair.

To Dad, we never told anything private or concerning house. Dad's was a one sided affair for us. It was he who was keeping this relation alive. We had no feeling or love left in our hearts for that man.

He made our sweet doll like Mom die inch by inch each day. He choked her voice. He dried up her tears, he ruined her youth. How could we forget and forgive him? No way.

I was assigned by my sister to tell Mom regarding my sister's decision to live with her lover from next month.

That day Mom was on her silence fast in which she remained quiet all the day long. Mom had become a staunch religious lady. She passed her time by visiting yoga classes, meditation camps and religious discourses.

Mom was calm that day.

Hesitantly I told her, 'Mom, I want to tell you something about Shikha.'

Mom made a sign with her hand smilingly signaling me to carry on. With this gesture I was trembling to say that horrible thing. It seemed Mom knew everything going on in this house. We thought she didn't bothered but it seemed she had deep concern for us.

My sister had told me that the people who are deeply religious come to know everything about their dear people, be it present, past or future.

That's why my sister was hesitant telling Mom all about her, herself fearing lest Mom may predict anything obnoxious or inauspicious about her lover. Then they won't lead a normal married life.

Mom was mistrustful about the marriage of her daughters. May be she was wary of such things because she had no faith in the institution of marriage now.

Mom was a devoted wife to her husband and he didn't value her. Dad left her for a dark and young woman. Mom was dignified, she belonged to a rich family and she was not lacking in anything. Then also she failed. And that made her a firm believer in luck. She normally said we would get what God has written in our luck.

After all a marriage is what two people decide to make. When two people marry they have a hope that their marriage will last for ever. But normally this doesn't happen. Circumstances can worsen and things can go out of control. Most Marriages become corrupt and break up. Outside person intrude and create splits in nice couples.

History tells us that marriage is that exceptional and immortal social contract that has continued through all ages. It has proved successful in all cultures and communities. Marriage gives stability to our lives but at the same time some people are fearful of such stability in their personal lives.

We become fearful and wary to an unconditional surrender before our life partners. We become fearful to think that if the other person failed to value our surrender and privacy or didn't become worthy of our faith then where will we stand.

A marriage is a box of memories. If that box of reminiscences is full of sweet and comfortable recollections then the marriage can be called a success. A marriage is described as a trail of moments of happy togetherness and it is more important that which of those moments – sweet or bitter are stored and arranged like a beautiful album.

Now I have come to know that cracks appear in marriage due to petty things. To keep a marriage in tact the partners should avoid hurling harmful words on each others – words injure more sharply and deeply than knives.

We should not marry simply because every one else does it. We should not marry for children since any number of children can be adopted. To marry for an imaginary sense of gaining security is not wiser because no marriage can provide any guarantee.

In a marriage two strangers decide to live together for life and pledge to be together in the dim attraction of beauty and charms for each other.

For some cowards, marriage is a hazardous sport and for a few others it is foolish step. For other few it is a journey without any logic. Some admit that it is madness, a relief from depression, a stage of helplessness and a journey full of blind curves and uncertainties.

My sister had decided to go and live with her man without any ceremony, registration, pledge or witness.

She had this faith if they were destined to love and live together, no ceremony can be a hindrance and if they were doomed to fall apart, no strong ritual can save them.

Mom's and Dad's marriage was before us.

So much ritual and so many relatives were involved but they didn't have a day of delightful togetherness.

Mom told us that Dad stopped loving her a month after their marriage. They had a bad chemistry and a worse luck.

Now time had changed. Live-in relationships have come to stay. Old values had changed. The new generation is experimenting new ideas and it is ready to take risks.

Dad had broken apart from his mistress.

Mom was in a state of unpleasant unhappiness and she had become neutral and dispassionate.

My brother got a good job in America and was settled there. He had no interest coming here. Me and my sister were mature enough to go for matrimony. We were fast losing our glow and sheen.

At this point a woman makes a last forceful attempt to find a husband for her. Her hair start graying, her body becomes plump and her worries multiply as she starts sliding beyond 35. Eligible men lose interest in her as the shelf life of a women is much shorter.

My sister would say, 'what to do now. For the last so many years I have been postponing the issue. The circumstances of this house won't improve. Mom belongs to another world. Dad has created complications with his second marriage. Who will think or worry about us. We will have to settle our matter ourselves.'

She was of this view that there is no limit in love.

There is no value of love as compared to marriage. The person who doesn't understand love is shortsighted. Life can't run simply by bare needs and feelings. There should be sensitivity, passion and liveliness in relationships. And a commitment to each other is essential precondition for love.

I asked Mom, 'Sikha is shifting. The boy is from a nice family. They know each other well. Let us pray she is settled well. Time has changed now. Moreover she has a brilliant job. I don't think she will get into any trouble.'

The silence of Mom said it all.

Without any scuffle with the older generation and without any ceremony or formal farewell my sister shifted to their flat - both invested in that.

I was there to look after Mom.

My brother settled in America. He too couldn't decide to marry. He had seen the unhappy marriage of Mom and Dad. He also formed this view that a marriage is a nonsense affair.

I was looking up an appropriate time to tell Mom about my love. I was looking forward to the day when I too would shift to Nikumb's house one day.

My love had made me selfish and self-centered. I started thinking that I could not live without Nikumb. I was forgetful of everything but he was with me in my every moment. My life seemed to stop there. I could see no further.

I was a novice in the matter of love. I wanted to fly in the sky but I didn't know the way. I don't know why I fell madly in love with him. Once love came in, everything else took a back seat. No logic, no reasoning, no second thoughts. He was worth more to me than mere love.

My lover would tell me that I was very sexy and gorgeous. I had a great body. Well developed breasts are in reality a looming knell in a girl's neck. It enhances her value in the eyes of those men who want her for their lust and want to make her their rubber doll. The beauty of girl is worthy when it has the power to pull a man towards her. The day her breasts lose firmness, men run away and when these breasts dry up, men totally desert her.

I was so thrilled to see myself married off. I didn't care what he was. I was every kind of woman. I was single, I was an old maid, I was a virgin, I was a wicked and I was an unmarried wife. And I preferred the last. I was already an old maid – in my thirties. My sister always warned me about turning into an old maid. She said if I didn't stop wearing slacks and start perming my hair, I would turn into an old haggard woman before I knew it.

Out of unease and inquisitiveness, I would advance two steps forwards but then due to fear and apprehensions, I would retract back too soon.

I was passionate to reach my destination but how could leave my Mom alone on her own in that large house. She was not in a good state of heath and mental make-up. She spoke little. If I would go, she would perish soon.

Life was going in a routine way but I was heading towards maturity.

My lover was a man of today – a carefree metro sexual. He was against the institution of marriage. I could not preserve my virginity. In fact he wanted it from me for him. It was his precondition for my companionship. No lifelong commitment – we'll stay together till love and faith last between us.

He was an expert in making love. He would take me to the zenith of sexual proximity, we would stay there for long and then with skilled strides we would calm down and come to our own selves. I would float on top of the world. He would direct the whole act so deftly and expertly.

His control on him was marvelous. He would take me to his gracious bed room. He would take out all my clothes slowly, steadily, collectedly and tenderly. He loved me in an amazing fashion reaching to every pore of my body. There was no hurry or nervousness or urgency on his part.

He felt and touched my body in such a way as if I was the most expensive thing of this world. Together we would sail in our sensual feat. He would take me to the highest point of enjoyment. At right place he would pause and waited for me to reach near and equal him. His concern for me was remarkable. Together we would attain orgasm. When he was released, he kept himself there for long.

Time changed too quickly for me this time. There was a time when I was deeply in love.

Then I lost my love. And my faith in love was gone.

Now I don't know much about love. It has lost its appeal, charm and veneer for me.

I hate it now. I laugh when I watch a movie depicting a true and sacrificing love story. I wonder how can someone take his own life just for the sake of love.

These are all concocted tales meant for our momentary entertainment. Writers get paid to popularize these nonsense and impractical fantasies.

Love has burnt many houses; it has broken millions of hearts and it led numerous youth astray.

Love stands nowhere in the test of time. It is an abstract thing, beyond comprehension of ordinary people. Love means foolishness and stupidity for a man struggling to make a provision for his daily bread for the day long.

Love is a fool's paradise. A wise person doesn't get caught in its net. He knows it is foolishness to bear its pangs unnecessarily.

Love is not passion. Passion is more forceful and enduring. It encourages man to do or die. It is more enduring and more humane feeling.

Instead I am quite familiar with lust. I am comfortable with it. There are no unnecessary strings attached to it.

I was not like my sister. She was a sentimental fool trying to seek faithfulness from her lustful lover who was already married. Love, faith, trust, loyalty - all these things have become a thing of past.

Leave that, Money is the modern concept.

Mom sought divorce to be happy. She gets her monthly maintenance cheque in time. What else she wants?

When her husband is giving her a lot of money, she should not ask any ifs or buts, she should just enjoy.

One should not think much. Thinking too deep creates complications. Your face would get wrinkled.

A woman smart enough should not worry for relations especially with men. A man is like a dog. Man is very erratic and fickle. Whosoever cuddles him, hugs him and throws before him a piece of flesh, he belongs to him and wags his tail in front of him.

For centuries, man has thought his woman primarily an object of sex. All battles are fought either for power or for enslaving more and more beautiful women.

When a man grabs power, he makes a harem and appoints numerous eunuchs to safeguard it.

Expecting fidelity from a man is a folly. We women should train ourselves to outsmart men. Set your eyes on a steady income and then fuck the bloody life in a thousand ways.

Blaming fate or your adulterous man is no solution. That complicates the things further. Forget the future and bury the past. Whosoever doesn't love you at present, kick him out. Why find fault with everyone?

I don't blame anyone. Why should I?

I live in present and the present belongs to those who have courage to face the reality, those who have money and other resources.

My sister had no patience. her lover was like a lucky hen who lays a golden egg daily. It was easy to fleece and swindle him. What he wants at the most. Just place yourself under him.

But my sister was unskillful and tenderfoot. She was in a hurry. She could not wait and watch.

Life is a game of perseverance. A hurried man laments at his hasty decisions. I was lucky to have a pragmatic and straightforward approach.

I was thirty when my experienced friend gave me this valuable advice, 'a compromise is third rate option for an unfortunate and a fool. If you want anything, go for it and grab it. Life fucks a hesitant man more often. For a daredevil, it shows her ass easily. In life, think of a comfortable income first. After that you can enjoy life on your terms.'

She went on further, 'To get a steady income - work hard and equip yourself with good qualifications. But if you still fail, take a shortcut in life. Hook a man wealthy enough who may fulfill your wishes. If you live with him, you will be his queen and if he kicks you out, he will have to shell a lot of money to you as a compensation for the divorce. You will enjoy without him too. Life doesn't pull on with principles and morals alone.'

And she was right. Dad ditched Mom and she divorced him. Mom got a lot of money. She wept for him but for a brief period. Then she realized that by her living a wretched and sullen life, her husband won't come back and then she became practical.

Dad came seldom to her. He never fulfilled Mom's sexual needs. Mom needed love too. And love can't be enjoyed with any Tom, Dick and Harry.

I maintained my cool. I got this formula from my Mom. She remains calm and collected.

Every day is like a separate chapter of our life. Just like every page of a novel tells a different thing, no two pages are the same, so is life. Always moving and changing and thus opening new vistas and novel ways.

You never know which moment may unfold a chain of happiness and at which moment we get encircled by pains and sorrows. Both ups and downs are inseparable and are essential to make life meaningful.

If life becomes a perpetual and eternal pleasure then also it is hell, we will soon get bored. If we remain reeling in pain and troubles and there is no ray of hope or change, that too is an unending torture. When happiness comes after a spell of depression or failure, we thank God.

Yes, I was lucky to have a pragmatic and straightforward mother.

She told me one more thing too, 'Never ever come to me dejected or loaded with complaint. See the life in its eyes. What is today won't remain there tomorrow. When faced with a problem, don't cry. Think of options and alternatives. If a man walks over you, forget him. If he is happy, then why on the earth are you miserable and crestfallen.'

With my sister, Dad never had a scuffle regarding her lover. She revealed nothing of any sort to him. She never told Dad where she works or what she earns.

She told me once, 'Has ever this man showered his love on us when we went to school. He never attended our parent-teacher meeting, never took us out for any vacation. He is simply no body for us now. He is seeking solace from the same place where he played havoc with peace of us all. He lost his timing now. So forget what he says.'

I am a fool to spare a soft corner for Dad in my heart. Sometimes I too feel bad about Dad but his present pitiable condition disturbs me a lot. There is no one to look after him. He lives now with some old lady from his office. Such a high ranking, smart and intelligent officer lost everything because he had no control on his lustful desires.

Then I argue with myself - he has himself created that hell with Deepika. Deepika had sex with her and got pregnant. She wanted to trap him so firmly. Dad had a nice wife and sweet children. He spared no love for them and he spoiled their childhood.

When Dad learned about my relations with a married man whom he knew too, he had a heated discussion with me one day.

I spoke in the language of rebellion. Dad called him a vagabond and an unreliable fellow. I rebuked Dad's mistress who was currently involved with my Boss. Dad couldn't hear that. He slapped me.

I yelled at him and told him to leave me alone.

Mom was inside. Probably she listened all that or not. When Dad would come to our house Mom would slip away in neighborhood. She avoided Dad even in dreams.

Dad abused me, yelled at a high pitch.

Mom didn't speak a word. She had completely lost her tongue. She had so many scuffles with Dad that she preferred to keep herself completely out of all that humbug. She started chanting religious mantras in a low voice.

I was in a sticky situation. I couldn't go and live with my lover in his house. If I chose to go Mom would perish quickly. I was here and I took some care of her. I didn't leave my lover completely. We would meet after a week or fortnight and we would make love.

Mom died one day. She died in her sleep. Doctors called it brain hemorrhage. She was in excellent state of health but she had put a lot of pressure on her brain and that wrecked her completely.

Now I was alone in that big house. But I liked my company. I wanted to be alone.

Dad stopped coming to my place. My brother didn't bother to come back to India. We were not on speaking terms. He was in this misunderstanding that I was going to grab that costly house all for myself.

When Dad died due to heart attack in the same year, my sister who was in Canada came and consoled me.

I wanted to leave that nasty ghostly house. We negotiated with an Estate Dealer to give us the desired amount. My sister was rich. She didn't take a single rupee from that deal. In a month, she flew back to her place.

I was nearing 60 now.

My interests had changed long ago. I was not a good  religious as my Mom was.

I developed a clear perspective of people around me, what they want from me and what I expected from them. I have clear convictions and priorities.

No man is an island. We need this society and the portion of society around us should be an asset to look into our future. We need a glimpse of past but it is the future to which we move day by day. All forms of happiness are meaningful if we see some future in it.

I admit I led a carefree and happy life. That was only due to the fact that I didn't live in illusions. I did what I thought was best for me first.

I retired from my job. I had read much about an old age home, I applied and I got a seat here. Here I got so much love and warmth and a new zest to place myself for the service of needy people.

Here I discovered a new meaning of life.

Life is neither lived in past nor it is lived in present. Life is always lived in future.

For the first time I saw my future here.

The folk here are striving to make not only their own life meaningful and momentous but also they can spare time and resources for the poor and needy. In that way they are helping God to lessen the woes and cries from this world.

www.ingramcontent.com/pod-product-compliance
Lightning Source LLC
Chambersburg PA
CBHW061726130726
47996CB00006B/2515